The Lion's Paw

By Jane Werner Watson
Illustrated by Gustaf Tenggren

MERRIGOLD PRESS • NEW YORK

© 1959 Merrigold Press, Racine, Wisconsin 53402. Copyright renewed 1987. All rights reserved.
Printed in the U.S.A. No part of this book may be reproduced or copied
in any form without written permission from the publisher.
All trademarks are the property of Merrigold Press.
ISBN: 0-307-90961-1   MCMXCI

"Ow!" roared the lion.

"There is a thorn in my paw. Who will take it out?"

"Not I," said the solid rhinoceros.
"I am whetting my pointed horn."

"Not I," said the startled kudu.

"I am racing away from here."

"Not I," the tall giraffe whispered among the tip-top leaves.

"Not I," said the bouncing baboon.

"I am having too much fun."

"Who will take the thorn out?"
cried the crowned crane flying by.

"Not I," said the hippopotamus.

"I am snuffling in the mud."

"Not I," said the small striped zebra.

"I am kicking up my heels."

"Not I," said the bright-eyed monkey.

"I am swinging by my tail."

"Not I," said the big gorilla.

"I am scratching away my fleas."

"Not I," said the elegant gazelle.
"I am leaping across the veld."

"Will no one remove the thorn?"
called the ibis over the purple pool.

"Not I," said the slippery crocodile,
smiling a hungry smile.

"Not I," said the trumpeting elephant.

"I am taking a shower bath."

"Not I," said the leopard.

"I am slinking through the spotted shade."

"Not I," said the solemn buffalo.

"I have too much work to do."

"Who will help Lion?" cried the ostrich
over the desert sands.

"Not I," said the sulky camel.
"I am chewing my cud."

"Not I," said the swooping vulture.

"I'm busy hunting a meal."

"Not I," said the spotted cheetah.

"I'm too busy hunting, too."

"I will then," said the little mouse.

And do you know?

She did!